3/2019

#mz

Quiet

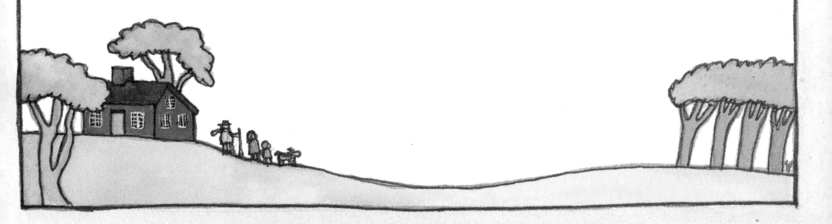

Quiet

TOMIE dePAOLA

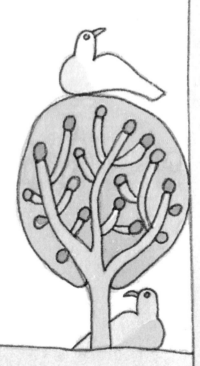

SIMON & SCHUSTER BOOKS FOR YOUNG READERS
New York   London   Toronto   Sydney   New Delhi

"My, oh my," the grandfather said.
"Everything is in such a hurry.

"The birds are flying so fast."

"And our dog is rushing after the ball," said the girl.

"I see a frog jumping high, into the pond," said the boy.

"And a dragonfly zooming over the water."

"Even the trees are waving their leaves.

"Busy as busy can be.

"Let's not be so busy.
Why don't we sit here,
you next to me.

"The birds are just like us.
Taking a rest, singing their song."

"Our dog is tired. I think he's dreaming."

"The frog is sitting and blinking."

"The dragonfly has stopped beating its wings."

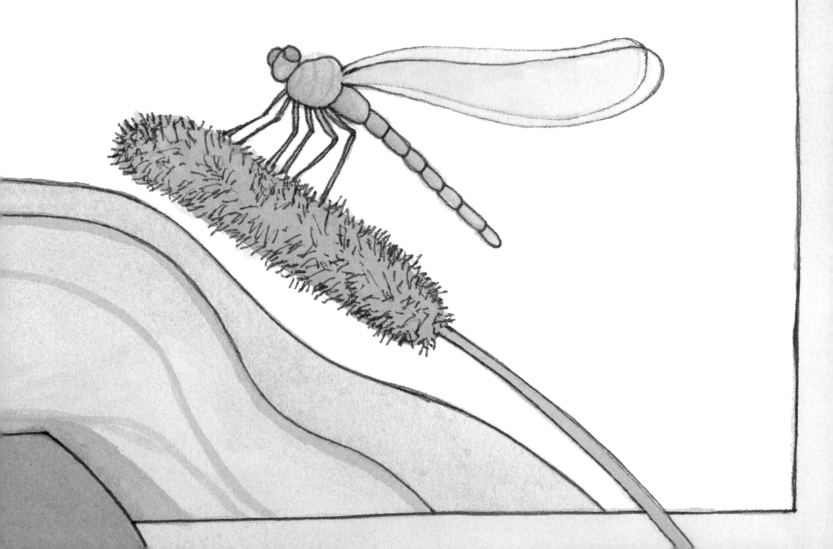

"Let us be quiet, like all our friends.
Quiet and still."

"I can think, when I'm quiet."

"I can see, when I'm still."

To be quiet and still is a special thing.

For all those who know the beauty of QUIET—
and pass it on to others

SIMON & SCHUSTER BOOKS FOR YOUNG READERS
An imprint of Simon & Schuster Children's Publishing Division
1230 Avenue of the Americas, New York, New York 10020
Copyright © 2018 by Tomie dePaola
SIMON & SCHUSTER BOOKS FOR YOUNG READERS is a trademark of Simon & Schuster, Inc.
For information about special discounts for bulk purchases,
please contact Simon & Schuster Special Sales at 1-866-506-1949 or business@simonandschuster.com.
The Simon & Schuster Speakers Bureau can bring authors to your live event.
For more information or to book an event, contact the Simon & Schuster Speakers Bureau
at 1-866-248-3049 or visit our website at www.simonspeakers.com.
Book design by Laurent Linn
The text for this book was set in Write Regular.
The illustrations for this book were rendered in transparent acrylics and colored pencil
on Arches 150 lb cold-press 100% rag paper.
Manufactured in United States of America
1118 PCH
2 4 6 8 10 9 7 5 3
Library of Congress Cataloging-in-Publication Data
Names: DePaola, Tomie, 1934– author, illustrator.
Title: Quiet / Tomie dePaola.
Description: First edition. | New York : Simon & Schuster Books for Young Readers, [2018] |
Summary: While observing the busy world around them, two children and their grandfather take a moment to appreciate being quiet and still.
Identifiers: LCCN 2017008358 | ISBN 9781481477543 (hardcover) | ISBN 9781481477550 (eBook)
Subjects: | CYAC: Quietude—Fiction. | Grandfathers—Fiction.
Classification: LCC PZ7.D439 Qui 2018 | DDC [E]—dc23 LC record available at https://lccn.loc.gov/2017008358